MAN OF THE HOUSE

FILTHY RICH LOVE

SADIE KING

LET'S BE BESTIES!

A few times a month I send out an email with new releases, special deals and sneak peeks of what I'm working on. If you want to get on the list I'd love to meet you!

When you join you'll get access to all my bonus content which includes a couple of free short and steamy romances plus bonus scenes for selected books.

Sign up here:
authorsadieking.com/bonus-scenes

MAN OF THE HOUSE

A billionaire recluse comes out of hiding to claim his curvy girl.

Jonathan

I haven't left the estate for seven years until Chloe
turns up at the gates.
She's full of smiles and wonder and every good thing in
this world that I'm not.
I can't keep my eyes off her. I watch her through my
bank of cameras, my window to the world.
But if she saw me, if she knew what I really was,
she'd run.

Chloe

No one ever sees the reclusive owner of Tanner
Hills, but he sees everyone.

The feeling of being watched is thrilling. Then he
speaks to me.

From the moment I hear his voice, I'm in love. It's
deep, it's demanding, and it's making me want to do
dirty things…

Man of the House is a short and steamy age gap billionaire romance featuring an OTT alpha male who isn't afraid to take what he wants and an innocent curvy girl.

1

CHLOE

I'm being watched.

I know it suddenly and with certainty by the prickly feeling at the back of my neck. I squint up at the wrought iron gates in front of me. The elaborate twirls and swirls meet at the top to spell out "Tanner Hills." The name of the mansion that sits, in its all red-bricked elegance, on the other side of the biggest, most intimidating gates I've ever seen.

There's a movement at the top where the gate meets the wall, a security camera swiveling around to get a good look at me.

My blouse is tight against my chest and my skirt's too short, but it's too late to adjust them now. I stare up at the camera defiantly. When you're filling in for the person who's filling in, you have to take whatever size uniform you're given, and they didn't have one that fits my curves.

The intercom crackles. "State your business."

The voice is deep and authoritative and sends a thrill down my spine.

"I, ah, I'm from the agency."

I wince inwardly at how squeaky my voice sounds in comparison. I cough and try again.

"Jenny's sick, and ah, Lisa's on holiday, so they sent me."

"What's your name?" the voice asks. It sounds like a lion purring, all deep and low and rumbling.

"Chloe." I lick my lips nervously and wait.

A minute ticks by, and there's nothing more from the intercom. I can feel the camera still watching, so I straighten my back and wait patiently, hoping whoever's behind that swiveling camera doesn't clock me for the fraud I am.

I'm not even supposed to be here. But Mom's getting worse, so for the last week I've shown up at the cleaning agency in Temptation Bay hoping they'll give me work. They service the mansions of Cod Cove, which is a short bus ride, and many stations of increasing wealth, up the coast.

I could tell something big had gone down this morning because they were all in a panic, calling everyone on the books in desperation until they turned to me.

I got a lecture on manners and professionalism and all sorts of stuff that seemed a bit much for someone going to a cleaning job, even a 19-year-old with no experience. No "formal" experience as I kept getting told, as if cleaning up after one of Mom's treatments doesn't count as cleaning experience.

But now that I'm here, in front of Tanner Hills Mansion, while a stranger behind a camera lens judges me, I'm not feeling so certain.

A few minutes pass and I'm about to give up, turn around, and go home. Then I think of Mom and how pale she was this morning. I reach for the buzzer. But before I can press it, the gates swing silently open, which I guess means I passed the first test.

I'm doing a little dance on the inside as I walk down the tree-lined avenue to the mansion. I can't shake the feeling that I'm still being watched. Some people might find that weird, but it makes me quiver in a delicious way, knowing the owner of that deep rumbling voice is watching me.

I glance up, looking for cameras, and spot one on a lamppost. They're the old-fashioned kind of lampposts that look like something out of a black and white movie, black wrought iron with swirls to match the gate, positioned at intervals from the gate to the house.

This whole place is beautiful, and I stop to take it all in. It's a million miles away from the two-bedroom apartment I left this morning.

I look up and grin at one of the cameras, because who wouldn't smile living in a place like this? Then I remember I'm here to work, and I'll probably get fired if I don't get to the house and start cleaning.

.   .   .

The door has one of those big brass knockers, and I can hear the knock echo on the inside as I let the brass strike the door. I straighten my hair and smooth my skirt, ready to meet the man behind the voice. My heart's racing as the door swings open.

"Oh." I try to hide my disappointment.

It's a middle-aged lady in a knit skirt and sensible cardigan. "Are you from the agency, dear?"

She's smiling so sweetly I feel bad for feeling disappointed. But I am disappointed. I wanted to meet the owner of the voice, but I suppose the residents of Cod Cove don't answer their own doors. "Yes, I'm Chloe."

"Come on in, Chloe. I'm Mrs. Hughes, the Estate Manager."

She ushers me inside and starts chatting about where the cleaning supplies are. I'm trying to listen, but I can't help but stare at the ornate staircase that takes up half the entryway.

It's beautiful, one of those ones you see in the movies with twin spirals that meet in the middle. The marble is speckled with gold, and a lush strip of burgundy carpet runs down the middle.

Mrs. Hughes hands me a duster. I follow her up the staircase and can't resist reaching out a hand to trail a finger up the velvet-lined banister. My finger sinks into the plush fabric, making my nerve endings jump to life.

Mrs. Hughes stops before a closed door on the second floor. She fixes me with a stern look that makes me feel guilty, like she knows I haven't really been listening.

"The man of the house is... quite particular," she says in a low voice. I lean in to hear her. "He likes things just so."

'Just so' could mean anything to the kind of person who lives in a place like this. "What do you mean?"

Mrs. Hughes presents an air of practiced efficiency and she speaks quickly, like I'm not the first cleaner she's given this speech to.

"Dust around objects, don't touch them. If you must pick something up, put it back exactly where it was." She holds her finger up on the word "exactly" to give it emphasis.

"Does he have OCD?"

Mrs. Hughes frowns and I'm worried I've offended her, but I'm thinking of my cousin who can't leave the house unless everything is in its proper place.

"He's particular," she says again.

I think about the gravelly voice and wonder exactly what kind of man I'm working for. "Is he in today?"

She laughs. "He's in every day." I must look confused, because she continues.

"He hasn't left Tanner Hills in seven years."

Before I can respond, she opens the door and ushers me inside.

"Will I see him?" I ask, feeling nervous and a little thrilled that this deep-voiced man, who's particular about the way he likes things done, might be prowling the halls while I clean.

She shakes her head.

"No one sees him." She turns to go, and before shutting the door fixes me with a look.

"But he will see you."

As my eyes adjust to the gloom, I discover I'm in a sitting room. At least I think that's what it's called. I've never been in a mansion like this. The entire room is bigger than the apartment I share with Mom.

There's a chaise longue at one end covered in crushed black velvet and set on golden legs. Two matching armchairs face it with a black marble coffee table in the middle. Another set of armchairs are in front of a fireplace, which doesn't look like it's been used in a while judging by how clean it is. A huge bronze statue of a lion perches next to the fireplace.

The walls are lined with old portraits. There's a bookcase and a large mirror with a golden frame that leans against the opposite wall to the chaise longue.

I pull open the thick velvet curtains to the only window, and the gloom is immediately banished. With sunlight streaming in, it highlights a thin layer of dust particles on the surfaces. I lift my duster and get to work.

I'm running the duster around the edge of the mirror when the skin on the back of my neck prickles.

I'm being watched. The sensation travels all the way down my spine and the backs of my legs until even my knees have goose bumps.

I don't stop cleaning; I quite like the tingling sensation that makes my body heat.

I finish dusting the mirror and move to the mantelpiece.

A soft whirring sound comes from the top of the bookcase. I glance up and spot the camera following me. I flash it a smile. It's thrilling being watched. It makes me feel all fluttery, as if something exciting is about to happen.

There are a few ornaments on the mantelpiece, and I dust around them. Then I come to a photo frame that's fallen over on its face. I reach for it, and a voice makes me jump.

"Don't touch that." It's the sexy rumble I heard at the gates, and my heart races.

"Sorry," I say, not sure if he can hear me. I look around for a speaker and spot the intercom by the door.

"Don't move the photo frames," the voice booms.

There are a few more frames on the mantelpiece, and they're all flipped forward. I dust around them, leaving them face down as instructed and wondering what the owner of the gravelly voice looks like.

2

JONATHAN

My heart kicks at my ribcage and I lean forward, unable to take my eyes from the screen.

Ever since she turned up at my gate looking like a lost lamb, I've been unable to tear my gaze away from the woman currently dusting my sitting room.

Chloe, she gave her name as, and I roll it around on my tongue, liking how it sounds.

Chloe's hair is pulled back in a messy bun, and the uniform she's wearing is too tight for her curvy frame. Her pale arm sweeps the duster along the mantlepiece, showing chipped nail polish on fingernails bitten to the quick.

She smiles as she works but it's masking worry lines, the creases on her forehead out of place on a woman so young.

Chloe turns to the bookcase and smiles at the row of hefty tomes I bought for pure decoration. It's the smile that does it. I've been entranced ever since she entered my grounds, but the curve of her lips has my chest pulling up tight and one word echoing through my head.

Mine.

As soon as I think it, I know it to be true. This curvy goddess buzzing around my house with her duster in hand is mine.

She's smiling as she works, and her wide-eyed looks make her far too innocent for the things my mind is imagining doing to her.

A surge of protectiveness wells inside me. I want to protect her and hold her and hear her story.

Whoever she is.

I turn my head to glance at the other monitors, each one showing different rooms of the mansion. I'll never again get caught out like I did once. Now, I see everything that goes on in my house.

Mrs. Hughes is in the kitchen, notebook in hand, checking off a list of some sort. No doubt ordering supplies for the pantry.

"What agency did Chloe come from?" She doesn't even jump when she hears my voice. She's gotten used to how I work.

Mrs. Hughes slips the notebook into her pocket and crosses the room to speak into the intercom.

"Clean and Shine. The usual cleaner is ill, and the usual stand-in is visiting family. I can find someone else if Chloe's not adequate."

Oh, she's adequate. More than adequate.

"That won't be necessary."

I type the company name into my computer and call the number that comes up. A chirpy woman answers.

I have a brief conversation with the agency, and they happily hand over her personal details. Chloe Davidson, nineteen years old.

Relief foods me when I find out her age. She looks so damned innocent I had to check.

She finishes the sitting room and moves to the first bedroom. I keep an eye on my girl, watching her work as I dare to dream.

If I was a different man, I'd stalk down there and introduce myself, charm her and take her out like she deserves.

But I'm not that man. And so I watch.

It's better this way. To watch from afar and imagine a life I'll never have with Chloe.

There's only one thing I can offer her, and I'm not yet that far gone to suggest what I want to do to her on her first day of work.

Too soon the day is over and she packs away her cleaning equipment and strolls down the long driveway.

My heart goes with her as she slips through the gate and heads into a world in which I no longer belong.

3
CHLOE

"Tell me again like I'm five, because I don't understand how you're in love with this guy from the sound of his voice."

Ashleigh eyes me skeptically, and I hand her over the milkshake we're sharing. "A sexy voice, Ash, the sexiest, growliest voice you've ever heard."

She takes a long sip of the milkshake and stares at me hard. "You sure it's not the massive mansion and billions of dollars he purportedly has that you're in love with?"

I kick my foot against the concrete sea wall we're sitting on and look out to the ocean. It's hard to explain to my best friend how I felt today. That it wasn't the golden gates or the perfect lawn or the massive house, it was the way his voice made me feel. A complete stranger. If he'd asked me to do anything with that voice, I would have. The question of his obvious wealth didn't even cross my mind.

"What do I need with his money?" I ask with an ironic smile as she hands me the milkshake back. The milkshake we're sharing because we're both poor.

The smile doesn't last long. The truth is I need money badly for Mom's meds. But I'm not so desperate that I'd compromise myself for the cash.

I'm telling Ashleigh about Mr. Tanner because this is a pipe dream. I've got a crush on my employer because he's got a sexy voice. It's not like anything will even happen.

"How is your mom?" Ashleigh asks gently, sensing the change in tone.

I think about how I left Mom this morning, pale and weary, the blanket pulled around her as she sat stoically in front of the TV.

"The same." I swing my legs up and push myself to a standing position. Mom will need me to get the dinner going soon and give her a bath.

"How about you? How's the job hunt?"

Ashleigh tells me about an interview she has next week in town in the marketing department of some big corporation. She doesn't sound too enthusiastic about it, but we've all got to work.

Her real passion is drawing. But any career like that is out of reach for people where we come from. We have to be practical around here, get a job and earn money to live any way we can.

I'm not complaining, it's just a fact of life.

We continue our walk along the waterfront,

heading away from Temptation Bay and to the crumbling apartment building where we both live.

A figure huddles over a small table outside the Something Fishy café. I recognize Ula in her gram's brightly colored robes and colorful beads. The table is set slightly away from the café and covered in a bohemian tablecloth.

She's searching for business and dressed up for the part. It's usually Ula's grandmother reading fortunes for tourists along the waterfront, but Ula's taken over since her gram got sick.

"Hey." Ula smiles as we approach and gestures for us to sit.

We've known Ula since we were kids, and she knows we don't want a reading. But her keen eyes don't miss anything.

"You're glowing, Chloe." She smiles at me knowingly and grabs my hand in hers.

A warm feeling comes over me, and I remind myself I don't believe in fortune telling.

Ula and her gram have been a fixture of Temptation Bay since as long as I can remember. They read cards and fortunes for tourists. I don't believe in the card reading and fortune telling they do for tourists, but I don't judge. We've all got to earn a living somehow.

But the way Ula's looking at me as her firm fingers run over my hands has me questioning my skepticism.

"You've met someone," Ula pronounces, her green eyes sparkling.

Ashleigh rolls her eyes, always the skeptic. "It's

obvious from the way she practically skipped over here that she's met someone."

Ula lowers her glance to my palm and spreads my fingers open, studying the lines there. "An older man," she proclaims.

I share a look with Ashleigh, and we giggle. I'm not sure how old my boss at Tanner Hills is, but the thought of the owner of that deep gravelly voice makes me squirm in my seat.

"It's a time to be bold," Ula says, giving her voice the eerie tone I've heard her grandmother use on tourists. "It's a time to take risks."

Ula frowns and goes still, her finger pressed to my palm.

I sit forward, all skepticism forgotten. "What is it?"

She shakes her head slightly and drops my hand. "Nothing."

The drawn out vows of the fortune teller are gone, and once again she's the childhood friend we grew up with.

"You want to get some chips and walk out to the pier?" she says brightly.

But the smile is too bright, and it sends a chill through me.

"What is it, Ula? What did you see?"

Not that I believe in palm reading or tarot or any of that, I tell myself. But there's no denying Ula and her grandma have some kind of gift.

They're the ones boarding up their caravan

windows before anyone else knows there's a storm coming. They're always down at the waterfront first when a fishing boat doesn't come back. And her gram took herself off to bed even before they diagnosed the cancer in her.

"It's nothing." Ula stacks the pack of worn cards and slides them into her bag.

She goes to pull the tablecloth off the table, and I stop her hand. "It's not nothing. Tell me."

Ula sighs and looks at me hard. I stare back defiantly, and her expression softens. "There's a shadow over him."

Her words make me shiver. "Over who?" My voice comes out as a whisper; I already know who she's talking about.

She pulls the tablecloth off the table and folds it into a neat square. "This man you've met. He's in shadow."

"What does that mean?"

She stuffs the tablecloth into her bag and shrugs off the colorful robe. "It means he's hiding something."

She sees my confused look, because she puts a hand on mine. "It's not always bad. He could be masking something for a good reason. Just be careful, that's all."

I tell myself again that I don't belove in fortune telling and Ula's just being dramatic. But long after I say goodbye to my friends, the feeling of foreboding keeps nagging at me. Questions tumble around my head that I have no answers for.

What does the man behind the voice look like? How can I feel so much for someone I've never seen? And what is it he's hiding?

16

4

CHLOE

The next day I'm back at Tanner Hills. The cleaning job was supposed to be twice a week, but the agency called. The mysterious man of the house requested I come back.

So here I am, following Mrs. Hughes up the staircase and back to the room I was in yesterday.

"Did I miss something?" I ask as she holds the door open for me. The bronze lion statue snarls at me from its place by the empty fireplace.

I dusted this room from top to bottom yesterday, but Mrs. Hughes just holds the door open for me, her expression not giving anything away.

"He instructed me to start you off in here."

I open my mouth to question what I should do when every surface is dust free, but the stern look on her face makes me pause.

I'm getting paid to dust an already dust free room. It's an easy gig. I shouldn't complain.

Instead I put on a bright smile and breeze into the room.

Mrs. Hughes shuts the door behind me, and the only sounds are her fading footsteps and the ticking clock above the mantlepiece.

I hold my breath, wondering if he will speak to me today. So far it's been silence. The gate swung open as I approached, as if someone had been waiting for me. Then Mrs. Hughes met me at the door and led me here.

My skin prickles, and even though I'm entirely alone, I have the feeling again of being watched.

I remember where the cameras are and raise my hand and give them a friendly wave and a big smile. May as well let him know I know he's watching.

"Hello Chloe." I gasp at the sound of my name on his lips, deep and sexy and penetrating like nothing I've heard before.

My skin heats, and there's a flush of dampness between my legs. My heartbeat thunders in my ears, and my knees feel week.

"Hello..." I don't know his name so I settle on the first thing I can think of. "...sir."

There's a growl down the intercom, and it sends a new surge of wet heat to my panties. I'm getting turned on by a voice, which is ridiculous. I need to focus on my work, not on fantasizing about what the man behind the voice looks like.

I raise the duster and begin my work.

I start at the mantlepiece, going over every ornament and photo frame that I dusted yesterday, pushing my duster between each item and then running it along the sides of the fireplace.

As I work my neck prickles, and I know he's watching.

I'm in the same too tight uniform as yesterday, and it thrills me to think of him watching it ride up my thighs every time I reach up to dust. I shouldn't feel that way, but there's something naughty and delicious in what I'm doing. If Mr. Tanner is watching, then I may as well give him a show.

My heart's racing by the time I get to the last item by the mantelpiece, the statue of a lion, its jaws open in a roar. I dust its feet and have to reach up to get all of the statue. My skirt rides up, tickling the backs of my thighs, and I blush knowing he's still watching.

"Spread your legs."

The command is so powerful it stops me in my tracks. I pause with the duster in my hand and my heart hammering against my chest, not sure I heard him right.

"I said, spread your legs."

The audacity of his command makes me gasp. I should run. I should throw down the duster and get out of this mansion and away from a man who thinks he can command my body. But I don't.

Ula's words ring in my head *It's time to be bold.*

A delicious shiver makes my body heat with desire. I obey the voice and step my feet apart, as wide as the tight skirt will let me.

"Dust the lion again."

A thrill runs through me like an electric shock. I reach up, and this time with my legs spread my skirt rides up higher, giving the camera a perfect view of my bare thighs. A warm shiver spreads up my legs and into the hot place between. I take my time going over the lion, running the duster through the gaping mouth while I wait for his next instruction.

"Take your blouse off."

The command is outrageous. I should be racing out the door, down the staircase and out through the gate. But instead my trembling hands ease open the buttons, and I wriggle out of my too tight blouse. Thank God I put on my good bra today. It's white and lacy and just barely contains my oversized boobs. They push up over the top of the bra, and I'm aware that they're heaving as I try to get my breathing under control.

I'm standing half-naked in the middle of a room while a complete stranger feasts his eyes on my body.

I've never done anything like this before. I've never even been with a man. It feels so wicked and so delicious and so right.

"Dust the bookcase," he commands.

I do as instructed, looking for a second camera in the room. I find it over the curtain rail near the mantelpiece, facing the other side of the room where the bookcase is.

The bookcase has rows of old books that don't look like they've ever been read. I run the feather duster over the leather-bound volumes and thrust it into the crevices.

"Now the bottom shelf."

I start to crouch down, but he stops me with his voice.

"Bend over to dust it."

Wow. A flush of wet heat gushes in my panties, and my thighs quiver so hard I might collapse. His voice commanding me has my body on fire.

I bend down slowly, making sure my legs are spread and my ass faces the camera.

I slot the duster into the lower shelf and run it slowly over the books. As I come up, I run the duster up my legs and under my skirt. I hear a groan from the intercom, and I smile, knowing I'm turning this strong-voiced stranger on.

"Go and sit on the chaise longue." His voice is croaky like he's having trouble getting the words out.

I do as instructed, sinking into the plush fabric. It caresses my skin, and I run a hand up my legs to the hot place between.

"Lift your skirt, and don't move."

JONATHAN

I watch Chloe. I've been unable to take my eyes off her since she turned up half an hour ago. I thought yesterday was an anomaly, a lonely man latching onto the first pretty woman who comes into his house. But I spent a restless night, tossing and turning and thinking about the innocent-looking girl with the sweet smile and wide hips.

I don't understand why my heart squeezes every time the camera shows me her face, but I know I had to see her again. All of her.

She's full of smiles and wonder and every good thing in this world that I'm not. It makes me want to scoop her up and protect her from this wicked world.

It also makes me want to do indecent things to her. To take that sweet innocent mouth and wrap it around my throbbing member.

I'm watching her sit straight and expectant on the chaise longue, waiting for my command like a good girl. My dick twitches in my pants, wanting to be let out. I don't even know this woman, but I want to make her mine.

"Lay down," I tell her. "And spread your thighs."

I switch camera views so I'm looking down at this angel who's fallen through the gate and right into my living room. Her dark hair streams across the cushion behind her.

As she opens her pale legs, I catch a glimpse of white cotton panties. I'm rock hard. I have been since I saw her staring up at me by the gate yesterday, her white blouse pulled tight against her straining breasts. I wanted to reach down the camera and rip the buttons right off to see the flesh underneath.

Now I ache with want and the need to possess her. She's trembling like a newborn lamb, and I tell myself to go slow. Every part of me wants to race into the room, rip off those panties, and claim my woman. But if I go down there now, she'll take one look at me and run a mile.

Instead I pull out my aching dick and run my hand down the shaft. It only makes me ache for her more.

"Touch yourself," I tell her.

She runs a hand up her pale leg and strokes the white triangle of fabric. Her head tilts back, and her lips part in a silent moan.

I silently thank myself for getting the best cameras on the market as I see the detail of the fabric dampening underneath her fingers. God damnit, I want to bury my face between her legs, breathe in her scent, taste that sweet fresh pussy.

A bit of pre-cum dots the top of my dick, and I rub it into the head as I watch her. My blood is racing through my veins. I push the chair back and stand up. I've put the camera on the bank of screens, and I'm surrounded by her image.

"Take your panties off."

Slowly, she hooks her thumbs under the fabric and glides her panties down her thighs and over her knees. She looks straight down the camera as she wriggles out of them.

The control panel on my left beeps. A red light starts flashing, but I ignore it. Whoever's trying to get hold of me can wait.

"Bend your knees up for me, baby girl," I tell her. "I want to see all of you."

Like a good girl she bends her knees, keeping her feet flat on the chaise longue. Her legs are wide open so I can see her beautiful pink flower. It's framed with dark hair that glistens with her juices. I long to lick it, to taste her, to make her mine. But she's probably a virgin, so I won't rush this for her.

"Touch your breasts," I tell her.

Immediately she obeys me, which is a turn on in itself. Her breasts are spilling out of her bra and she pulls the fabric down, releasing the white flesh. The dark nipples spring to attention as she runs a finger over herself.

She's got one hand on her pussy and one hand

tugging at a nipple. My hand's tugging at my dick and I'm close to coming, but I already know it won't be enough.

The switchboard pings again, and I glance over.

Fuck. It's Beijing. A message is flashing on one of the monitors. There's been a security breach in their network. *Fuck.* I silence the beeping and turn back to my baby girl.

"Put a finger in," I command, not bothering to hide the urgency in my voice.

She slides her middle finger inside herself, and the pink folds suck it in hungrily. The pressure builds in my cock, and I match my strokes to the rhythm of her finger sliding in and out of her glistening pussy.

I zoom in so my screens are full of her. The palm of her hand rubs against her sensitive nub. She's swollen and wet, and my God I want to sink into her so badly.

The beeping starts again, and I bring my fist down on the control panel. A button pops off and flies across the room, but the alarm goes silent.

"Come for me, baby girl," I command.

Her pussy tightens around her finger like she's been waiting for me to give the command. Her head tilts back and her mouth drops open as pleasure overtakes her. I let myself go at the same time, shooting my seed over the bank of screens and covering her image as she writhes underneath her hand.

I zoom the camera out so I can see all of her delectable body trembling through the orgasm.

The phones start to ring, and I push the mute button. I won't leave my baby girl like this.

I watch her sit up and look around as if she's waking up from a dream.

"You're a good girl."

She smiles, and my heart throbs along with my dick. She sits up and reaches for her panties.

"Leave those."

She does as she's told, straightening her skirt over her bare pussy.

"I have to go," I tell her, hoping she can hear the regret in my voice.

She nods at me, and I feel a pang at leaving her so soon. "But I'll be watching. And tomorrow I'll make you mine."

Reluctantly, I tear myself away to go deal with a cyber-security breach in Beijing.

6

CHLOE

I spend the rest of the day in a daze. I've never done anything like that with a man before. It feels so naughty and so delicious and so right all at the same time.

It's not like I've never had the opportunity. The boys who hang around the neighborhood, who I've grown up with, they let me know every time I walk past what they'd like to do to me. But they're just boys, and I'm not interested in a quick fumble with someone I used to play hide and seek with.

I want to give myself to a real man, a man with a deep voice like slow molasses. I've never even met the man of the house, but I'm falling in love with his voice.

I dust every room on the first floor, longing to hear him speak to me again, but the intercom remains silent. I still have the feeling I'm being watched, and I catch the cameras following me. It makes me feel safe, protected, knowing he's watching over me.

I sing as I work, old show tunes from the movies I watch with Mom on the TV. I feel like I'm in one of them and can't help twirling around with the duster as I sweep it over his beautiful house, which really does look just like a movie set.

I'm disappointed when Mrs. Hughes tells me it's time to go home.

I walk slowly down the driveway to the gate. The prickly feeling on the back of my neck tells me he's still watching. The fresh air sends a breeze up my skirt, tickling my bare pussy. It feels like how I imagine his fingers would, grazing over my wet hair. I'm breathing heavily just thinking about it.

I long for him to call me back, to make me his, to find some release for this fever he's put me in. But the gate slides silently open.

My elation from the day subsides as I get further away from Tanner Hills, and the feeling of being watched leaves as well. The sudden loneliness makes me shiver. I wrap my arms around myself. It's all I can do not to run back up the hill and throw myself on the gates and push the intercom just to hear his voice.

Then I think of Mom and feel guilty for stalling. She'll be needing her dinner and a bath. I push away all thoughts of my boss and head for home.

7

JONATHAN

atching Chloe disappear down the street, her arms wrapped around her tiny frame, makes me want to reach right into the screen and pluck her to safety. She's out there alone, unprotected.

Her retreating figure triggers something deep inside me. Blood pounds in my ears, my chest constricts, and I can't breathe.

She walks out of frame and I stand up, pushing the chair back so hard it hits the floor. I zoom in on the camera and swivel the head. It picks her up crossing the road at the bottom of the hill, and I can breathe again.

But two seconds later she's gone. Fuck. My baby girl out there in the world alone where any man can lay his eyes on her.

The thought of someone else watching her makes my blood run hot.

Chloe is mine.

I couldn't concentrate this afternoon trying to smooth over the Beijing security breach. I was drawn to her, flicking between screens as she dusted each room in the house.

While she was in the furthest bedroom, I stalked down to the sitting room and snatched up her panties, breathing in her sweet pungent scent.

My dick's aching to make her mine, and the blood pumping through my veins is crying out to her.

Now she's gone, and I can't stand the thought of her being out there for all the world to see.

I scan the monitors. The house feels empty without her tiny figure buzzing around the rooms. I don't have sound on my cameras, but I could tell she was singing as she worked.

I don't even know this girl, and she's got my head in a mess. Her luscious curves, her look of wide-eyed wonder, the way she moves, smiling and singing and dancing. She's like a ray of sunshine piercing straight through my frozen heart via my raging hard dick.

I'll go to her, I decide. I need to see her again, to talk to her, to make her mine.

Then I catch my reflection in a blank screen. My scars carve a chasm of darkness from my right eye down to my chin, rough crevices of blackness in the skin.

There was a fire eight years ago. A cooling system in a server room blew. Electrical fires are quick to start and hard to kill. The control room went up in flames.

Mrs. Hughes was trapped in a room on the other side. I ran in to help her and managed to get her through to safety. But as I was coming out, burning wires from the ceiling fell and whipped me across the face, branding my skin forever.

Mrs. Hughes has been my devoted housekeeper ever since.

I refused cosmetic surgery, letting the scars heal in a haphazard pattern. They're only on the right side. If you look at me on the left in profile, I'm a rugged, handsome man in the prime of his life. If I turn to the right, I'm a monster. Made to scare children on Halloween.

I've always kept to myself, more at home with binary and the languages of coding then with making small talk in polite society.

But suddenly I was thrust into the limelight. I was the eligible bachelor freak-show. The up and coming tech-millionaire turned monster.

A TV station offered me a deal for a dating show where women would try to win me over after only ever seeing my good side and my bank account. Then I would reveal myself to them at the end and see how many still wanted to marry me.

I turned it down. I turned them all down.

My hankering for a quiet life became more pronounced. I began to go out less and less. When I did go out, I would be walking on the street and children would start to cry, women would cross the road. I became increasingly reclusive.

I dedicated myself to my work. It allowed me to increase my fortune from millions to billions. Seven years ago, I bought Tanner Hills. I moved in and haven't left the gates since. I've got everything I need right here. Until now.

I scan the monitors until I find Mrs. Hughes talking to the chef in the kitchens.

"Mrs. Hughes," I say, making her jump, "bring the car around."

She throws a puzzled look to the camera above the door.

"Now," I bark. She turns quickly and marches out of the kitchen. I pick her up on a screen heading to the garage.

I may not have left the estate in seven years, but I keep a pristine Mercedes in the garage primed and ready.

It's out front and waiting when I descend the steps ten minutes later. The driver holds the rear door open for me, no trace of the surprise he must be feeling at being asked to do his job for once.

"I'll drive myself."

"Very good, sir."

It feels good to be behind the wheel again, the leather under my hands, the hum of the motor. The gates swing open and I drive over the threshold for the first time in seven years, in search of my baby girl.

8

CHLOE

 'm humming to myself as I come around the corner of the apartment block. The light's starting to fade, and I don't see Ryan at first.

"What ya singing?" he asks, stepping in front of me.

The smile instantly slides off my face.

"Let me past, Ryan," I say, sidestepping around him.

He shoots an arm out, blocking my way.

"What's a guy got to do to get some attention around here?" He pushes his freckled face right into mine, and I smell cigarettes and cheap beer.

"Stop being an asshole for starters."

He's so shocked that his hand drops to his side, and I slip past before he realizes I'm through. I'm usually timid and easy to bully, but I'm so hyped from today I feel like I could take on anybody.

"A potty mouth doesn't suit you, Chloe," he calls after me. But I'm already through the door and into my apartment.

. . .

"Good day?" Mom asks, her smile a little too bright. She's in her usual spot on the sofa, propped up by pillows, her legs resting on the coffee table. I wonder if she's moved at all since I left her eight hours ago.

"You take your meds?" I ask, checking the pill case on the coffee table. It's empty.

"Took the last lot hours ago, love." She checks her watch, and even the small movement of lifting her arm makes her wince. "Must be time for the night-time pills," she says hopefully.

"Not quite yet."

It's another three hours before she's due to take the evening dose, which will knock her out until morning. I wonder how long I can distract her before the pain becomes too much.

I start talking about my day as I make the dinner, describing the house and grounds in detail for her. She was too tired to hear about it yesterday, but today she needs the distraction, and she listens intently as I tell her all about the mansion. She asks about the man of the house, and I tell her he has a nice voice.

The memory of it causes a flush to creep up my neck, and Mom raises her eyebrows at me. She may be suffering silently through the pain, but she doesn't miss a trick.

After dinner I help her bathe and get her into bed. She's clenching her teeth at every movement, and so I get the night meds even though it's thirty minutes too early. She swallows them gratefully and lies back on the pillow, waiting for them to take hold. As she drifts off into a pain-free place, I clean up the dishes from dinner.

I've got my hands in a tub of soap suds washing the dishes when my neck starts to tingle. The hairs stand up, and a hot sensation travels down the length of my body.

I look up, and there's a black car with tinted windows parked across the road.

A plate slips through my hands and splashes into the sink, sending suds flying into my hair. I don't know how long the car's been there, but I know it's him.

My body's reaction is instant. The warm tingle spreads to the place between my legs, and I feel myself getting wet. My breath becomes shallow; even my nipples start to throb.

I'm trembling so badly I drop another dish. I can't help staring at the car, willing him to come inside and claim me. But the windows remain dark and unmoving.

Doubt starts to sneak into my mind. Maybe it's not him. Maybe it's just a car parked on the street. But no one owns an expensive car like that around here. And I just know, my body knows, that it's him.

I manage to finish the dishes without dropping anything else, and before I turn out the light, I give him a little wave. Even if he doesn't want to come in, it's comforting to know he's out there, watching.

Gentle snoring coming from Mom's room lets me

know she's asleep, and I pad into my own room. But when I lay down, it's like a fever raging inside me.

My body feels hot thinking about his voice telling me to do things. I turn over and try to breathe deeply, but I can't calm my needy flesh.

My hands trail over my breasts, which are warm with imagined heat. The nipples harden under my fingertips, and I conjure up the memory of his voice telling me to rub them. I want that voice, that mouth to wrap around my breasts.

I wet my finger and trace circles on the hard nipples, imagining it's his tongue. My other hand snakes lower to the fire between my legs. With his voice in my head, I bring myself to an easy climax.

But it's not enough. There's no relief. I know I won't feel satisfied until I can hear him again, touch him, feel him inside me.

My body's on fire and I turn from side to side, knotting myself in the sheets, unable to stay still, unable to sleep.

Ula's words haunt me. *"He's in shadow"* I wonder what it means.

I get up once in the night and peer out the window. The car's still there, unmoving. I watch it for a few minutes.

It's calming, knowing he's outside watching over me. My breathing starts to slow, and my body relaxes. I go back to bed and finally fall sleep.

· · ·

Mom's croaky voice pulls me out of turbulent dreams. I don't know how long she's been calling my name.

"Coming, Mom."

I shake the sleep out of my body and clamber out of bed.

Before I head downstairs, I throw back the curtain. The car's gone.

Disappointment hits me in the stomach, and I sit back on the bed. Then Mom calls again and I race down the stairs, trying to banish all thoughts of him.

It seems to take forever getting Mom dressed and fed and settled in front of the television. She's in a chatty mood, and a pang of guilt shoots through me for being so eager to get out the door.

I'm practically skipping when I arrive in front of the gates at Tanner Hills. I push the intercom with a big stupid grin on my face. The gates swing open immediately, and I get the familiar feeling that he's watching me.

Mrs. Hughes greets me at the door with a warm smile.

"He went out last night," she whispers to me conspiratorially. "First time in seven years."

A thrill runs through me at the confirmation of what my body already knew. It was him in the car last night, watching.

"The boss left specific instructions for you today." She hands me the feather duster.

"He wants you to clean the bedrooms in the eastern wing."

My stomach's going flippity-flip as she leads me up the grand staircase and along a corridor that seems to stretch forever. I'm sure his eyes are following me, and I can't help humming as I go.

"Start at this end and work your way back," she says, hustling me through the last door on the left.

I'm so impatient for her to leave that I almost push her out the door in my eagerness.

Once she's gone, I stand in the middle of the room panting in anticipation, waiting for him to instruct me. He doesn't disappoint.

"Start dusting."

The voice is deep and commanding, and my skin prickles with goose bumps at the sound of it.

The room is decorated in yellow and gold with floral patterns on the walls and upholstery. The furniture is sparse, just a bed, a fireplace, and a dressing table. It doesn't look like anyone's slept in here for a long time, or maybe not at all.

I'm not sure where he wants me to start, so I move to the dressing table. I run the feather duster lightly over the painted wood.

There are no sounds from the intercom, but I feel his eyes on me. Every swish of the duster sends a shock through my body as I wait for his next command.

"The fireplace."

I dutifully move to the fireplace and reach up to dust the mantle. My skirt rides up my legs, and the memory of yesterday sends a shiver right up my thighs.

I'm impatient for him to talk to me, to instruct me,

to demand something from me. But he leaves me to dust, working my way around the entire room until I'm squirming with anticipation.

After what seems like an age, the intercom crackles again.

"Leave this room," he demands "Enter the room directly across the hall and await instruction."

I almost run across the hall and pull open a heavy door. It opens to a room with black painted walls and thick grey carpet. A four-poster bed sits against the wall with a purple velvet throw covering the bed.

The only light's coming from an orange lamp on the bedside table. The smell of camphor and cologne fill my nostrils. It's a heady aroma, and I close my eyes and breathe it in deeply.

This is his room, I realize. His bedroom. My knees almost buckle beneath me, and I have to stop myself from sinking into the floor.

I feel like I've passed some kind of test, and I'm about to get my prize. As if on cue, the intercom sparks to life.

"Do you trust me?" the voice asks.

I nod slowly, my eyes searching for the camera. I find it above the bed and stare straight into it.

"Good," he says. "Lock the door."

There's an iron key in the lock, and I turn it until I hear the satisfying click.

My heart races as I wait for the next instruction.

"Take your blouse off."

My fingers tremble as I stumble over the buttons.

My hand brushes over a nipple, sending a tremor through me. The fabric slips down my arms and falls to the floor with a swish.

"Take your bra off."

I unhook the back and glide the straps over my arms. My breasts fall loose, and I hear an intake of breath.

There's a moment of silence.

"You're beautiful," he says. The voice has a croak to it, and I suddenly feel so hot knowing I can make this powerful man speechless.

"Take your skirt off."

I slowly undo the zipper and slide the skirt down my hips and step out of it.

Knowing he's watching me as I strip makes my body flush with heat. I'm burning for his touch, and I'm sure he must be able to see the wetness coming through my panties.

"Now your shoes."

I slip out of my shoes and sink my feet into the lush carpet. My senses must be on high alert, because even my toes start tingling as I wriggle them into the plush carpet.

There are just my panties to go, and then I'll be completely naked. My breathing is shallow, and I can feel my breasts moving up and down with every short breath. I want to touch them, to rub my nipples, but I dare not move without his instruction.

It's agonizing to wait, but it's an agony tinged with

deliciousness. Finally, he gives the command I've been waiting for.

"Take off your panties."

The voice makes me shudder with desire. I'm so wired with anticipation that I run my hands over my breasts on the way down to my panties.

He sucks in air, and a low rumble growls down the intercom. I gently pull down the fabric of my panties and step out of them so I'm standing naked before him. It feels wicked and sexy, and I feel so powerful knowing the effect I'm having on him.

I look up at the camera, my eyes wide and lips parted. Ready for the next move.

"Go to the table by the bed," he orders. "Put on what you find there."

My heart races as I move to the table. I run my hand over the dark polished oak and pick up a length of silky black fabric.

He must see my confusion.

"It's a blindfold. Put it on."

I hold the sleek fabric up to my eyes and tie it tightly behind my head. It's smooth and thick, and I can't see a thing through it.

"Do you promise that whatever happens next you won't take the blindfold off?"

I nod.

"Good girl. Stay exactly where you are."

There's a sudden coldness in the room, like he's not watching anymore. It's an empty feeling, and I almost cry out. Then I hear a creak and a scraping noise like furniture sliding on carpet.

The back of my neck prickles and I know he's back, but something's different. I hear breathing. He's in the room with me. The prickle spreads from my neck down my body and all the way to the tips of my toes.

I feel him moving around me and I turn my head, trying to find where he is.

"Good girl."

The voice comes from my left near my shoulder. I snap my head around, but he's staying just out of reach.

"Do you want me to touch you?" he asks.

Yes! My body is screaming, but I'm too tense to do anything but nod.

"You can speak to me; I can hear you now." He's closer now, and I feel the warm air on my neck, his voice a whisper in my ear. I nod again.

"I asked, do you want me to touch you?" His voice has a hint of impatience to it, and the power of it makes me whimper.

"Yes," I say, licking my lips. "Yes, sir."

9

JONATHAN

She's standing in nothing but the blindfold, her body quivering under my gaze.

"Do you want me to touch you?" I ask her again. I want her to speak, I want to hear her voice.

"Yes," she says. Her tongue darts out and licks her swollen lips.

"Yes, sir."

My dick trembles in my pants. It's the sexiest thing I've heard. I'm almost overcome by the urge to bend her over and claim her as mine right now. But there's something about the way she fumbled out of her clothes, all innocent and so fucking sexy that warns me to take it slow.

"Bend over and put your hands on the table."

She does as she's told, and I get the perfect view of her perfect round ass. Her skin glints golden in the lamplight, and I can't hold back any longer. I must touch her.

I run a hand over the buttock, around her stomach and up to her breast. Her skin's smooth as the silk blindfold she's wearing and warm as a summer's day.

She whimpers as I touch her, and I know she's enjoying this as much as I am. My cock pushes against my pants, and I have to undo the fly to let it out.

Her breast trembles under my touch, and I reach my other hand up until they're both sitting in my hands.

God, it's a beautiful sight. I'm standing right behind her bent over body, and I could easily slip my cock in and fuck her right here. But she's trembling like a leaf, and so I have to ask.

"You're new to this, aren't you baby girl?"

She nods once. Then she finds her voice. "I'm...not experienced." She says it quietly like she's ashamed, not knowing it's the best news I've had all day.

"You mean you're a virgin?"

"Yes," she says. "I'm a virgin, sir."

I groan as she says the words. I'll be the first man inside her, the first and the last to claim her. The only man she'll ever have.

"I'll take it slow," I tell her, and she nods, shaking her brown curls down her bare back.

"But I will demand things from you. Do you understand?"

"Yes."

"Yes what?"

"Yes, sir."

My God. I must get some kind of release soon or I'll

implode. But I'm a man of my word, and I'll take this slow for her. I'll take it so fucking slow she'll be begging me to fuck her.

I run my thumbs over her nipples, gently strumming them until her trembling stops and she's moaning with pleasure. A red flush creeps onto her neck and I lean forward and kiss her back, making sure to keep the scarred side of my facing turned away.

"Turn around."

She straightens and turns, standing before me like a patient goddess, her nipples dark and hard in the lamplight. In one quick movement, I pick her up and sit her on the side of the bed. She sinks into the velvet cover, and I kneel in front of her.

"Spread your legs."

Her thick golden thighs lead to a dark patch of hair that's slick with wetness and the pink folds beneath. I breathe in her earthy scent, and my dick protests against my pants. I give myself two long, hard strokes.

I'm aching to push into those folds, to let her pussy take my hard cock in its warm embrace. But instead I run my hands up her golden thighs and press my palm against her pussy.

She gasps when I touch her. I stroke her slowly until she relaxes, and I feel her wetness spreading on my hand.

I grab a handful of thigh flesh and press my lips to the delicate skin. She whimpers against me, and I move my mouth upwards until I have her pussy on my lips.

She tastes like heaven, sweetness and damp, and my mouth and nostrils are full of her.

She cries out as I devour her, my tongue claiming what's mine. I pull her buttocks towards me and lose myself in her sweetness.

She leans back on the bed, and the moans escaping her lips cause a bit of pre-cum to shoot out of my dick. I pull away for a moment, and she whimpers.

"Please..." She's leaning back on her elbows, breasts in the air and legs spread before me. Holy fuck, I've never seen such a glorious sight.

"Please what?"

"Please... keep going, sir."

I tug at myself while I lean in and lick her pussy, tracing slow circles on her clit with my tongue while one hand pumps my dick.

She's panting now as the pressure builds, and I pull harder, matching her rhythm. My dick's throbbing, and I almost can't stand it anymore.

She cries out and starts to shake, gushing sweet wetness over my lips. I shoot hot cum over her thighs, matching her orgasm. She's trembling again, but this time it's the climax running through her.

I wait till it subsides and then I push my tongue into her, licking up her juices. She responds immediately. Siting up, she wraps her hands around my head and pulls my face into her. Her fingers grab my hair, and she's rubbing herself against me as another orgasm shakes her body.

I give her a moment to let the pleasure course

through her. My dick gets hard again, thinking about all the ways I'm going to fuck her.

She untangles her fingers from my hair, and before I can stop her, she runs a hand down the right side of my face. I grab her wrist, but the way she goes dead still lets me know she's already felt the scar.

"What...?" she begins to ask.

"No questions!" I kiss her wrist and release her hand.

"I want to see you." Her fingers pull at the blindfold.

I snatch up both hands and pull her up from the bed. "No."

I grasp both wrists in my hand and ease the belt from my pants.

"You don't get to see," I tell her, guiding her to the bedpost.

She nods.

"Do you like what I've done to you, baby girl?" I ask more gently as I line her up against the bedpost.

She nods again.

"Do you want to keep going?"

She nods again, her mouth opens slightly below the blindfold.

"Tell me," I say, wrapping the belt around her wrists and looping it around the bedpost.

"I want more," she says, and I pull the belt tight. She gasps, arching her back and pushing her breasts out.

"Good. Because I haven't finished with you yet, baby girl." I take a nipple in my mouth and feel it harden under my tongue. Her pussy's soaking wet when I run my hand over it.

"I want..." she pants, the words lost in a moan as I rub her hard clit.

"You want what, baby girl?"

"I want you inside me," she says. "Please, sir, make me yours."

My dick throbs at the words, but I won't take her innocence like this. I won't have her finding out she gave her virginity to a monster.

"No," I tell her, and she whimpers.

I sink to my knees and hook her leg over my shoulder. My tongue flicks to her clitoris, and she's soon lost in her pleasure. I slide a finger into her pussy. It's tight and hot, and fuck! I want to fuck her so bad. I bring her to climax quickly so I can get that hot pink mouth wrapped around my dick.

"I'm going to untie you, and you have to promise to keep the blindfold on." She nods slowly, her breath still coming short from the last orgasm.

"Get on your knees," I tell her once I've untied the belt. "I'm going to put my dick in your mouth, and you're going to suck it."

She smiles at me like I'm giving her the best fucking gift.

"Yes, sir."

She grips the base of my cock and her tongue darts out, licking the head of my dick. She parts her lips and pulls me into her hot, wet mouth.

With the blindfold on, she has to feel her way

around me. She takes my balls carefully like they're fragile objects. The delicateness of it sends a hot rush of pre-cum into her mouth, and she gasps in surprise, then swallows it down.

From where I'm standing, her full breasts bob up and down as she kneels before me. With her eyes hidden, her pink mouth is accentuated, swollen lips wide open taking everything I'm giving her.

I wrap my hands around her head and pull her towards me. Her lips run down my shaft with every thrust. I pump her hard, fucking her mouth and watching her breasts bounce. She moans with every thrust and moves a hand to rub her clit.

She's as turned on as I am, and the sight of her touching herself while I fuck her mouth is too much. My dick explodes in the back of her mouth, shooting hot cum right down her throat.

She moans in pleasure and swallows my cum down, her own climax shuddering through her body. She holds me in her mouth until we both stop shaking, and I stagger back.

I bend down and kiss her lips, tasting my own salty cum and her sweet juices.

"You did good, baby girl." She smiles up at me, and my heart breaks a little bit. How can I ever show myself to this angel?

As if reading my thoughts, the smile turns to a frown.

"When can I see you?" she asks.

"You won't like what you see," I tell her.

"I don't care what you look like. I love how you sound; I love how you feel; I love how you taste."

Hope bursts forth in my heart. Maybe she would be different.

"Soon, baby girl, you can see me soon. But not today." I kiss her pouting lips.

"I'm going to leave now. But I'll be watching you."

She smiles again. "Will you watch over me tonight?" she asks.

"I'll watch over you every night, baby girl. Now start counting, and when you get to 100 you can take the blindfold off."

I dress quickly and slip out of the room.

10

CHLOE

'One hundred.' I pull the blindfold off, but I already know he's gone.

My body is tingling and tired, and I want to lie down on the bed and go to sleep. But instead I dress slowly, feeling a million miles away from the girl who did these same buttons up this morning.

The door still has the key in it, and I look around for another entrance. There must be a panel in the wall somewhere that's actually a door, but nothing seems obvious. Maybe it's a hidden entrance behind the fireplace.

This house really is like something out of the movies. I try pushing the fireplace and then the bookcase. But no hidden door is revealed.

Disappointed, I retrieve the duster from where I left it and venture out into the hallway. There's still work to do after all.

The next room is as sparse as the first and I work

quickly, singing to myself. My neck prickles in a familiar feeling, and it's comforting knowing he's there. He doesn't speak again, but I know he's watching.

A blush creeps up my neck under his gaze. This man has seen me, all of me. I opened myself to him like I've never done before, and I've never even seen him.

It was thrilling having a stranger touch me behind the darkness of the blindfold. Yet he didn't feel like a stranger. I felt a connection to him, not just in my body. I felt like I knew him already.

When my fingertips brushed over his scars, it didn't surprise me. I wanted to trace my hands over them, feel what he must look like. My man's worried I won't like the cut of his face, but he doesn't know I'm already in love with him.

I finish for the day and head out the gate. Once again, I feel bereft as I leave the safety of his watchful gaze. The further I walk away from Tanner Hills, the more the empty feeling grows, until it's gnawing at my insides.

By the time I reach the apartment block, I miss him so bad I feel sick to my stomach. So I don't notice Ryan stepping out in front of me.

"You don't look happy today, Chloe," he says. "Spend five minutes with me, and I'll put a smile on your face."

I brush past him, and he grabs my arm.

"Let me go!" I struggle but he's got me in a firm grip, his sweaty hands squeezing my arm. He pushes his face right into mine, and I smell hamburger breath that's tinged with cigarettes.

"I'll pay you," he says. "You need extra cash for your mom, right?"

I'm so shocked I can't move.

"Bet it costs a lot to keep up her meds." He tightens his grip. "There are a lot of guys around here who'd pay for a piece like you."

He laughs, and a fresh wave of meaty breath burns my nostrils.

Then he's being lifted and pulled off me by a pair of solid arms.

I didn't see the black car with the tinted windows pull up or hear the door swing open, and now a man, my man has Ryan by the neck.

"You. Dare. Touch. My. Girl." He aims a punch with every word, his strong arms rippling with every swing. He's holding Ryan by the scruff of the neck, and when he drops him, he slumps to the ground.

"Get up," commands my man, whose name I still don't know.

Ryan staggers to his feet.

"You touch my girl again, I'll kill you. Understand?"

Ryan nods, sending droplets of blood flying from his nose.

"Now get the fuck out of here."

Ryan bolts down the stairs, not daring to look at me as he runs past. My heart's racing as my man turns to face me.

He's tall, like basketball player tall, with broad

shoulders and thick arms. His hair is dark and shaggy, and his eyes are deep brown to match.

One side of his face sits perfectly, with a strong jawline, sharp and defined, and a hint of stubble grazing the jaw. The other side is scarred with deep slashes, the skin bunched in ridges and casting shadows onto itself. It's beautiful, like two sides of a coin, the gentle and the turbulent.

He's looking at me warily and panting from the beating he's just dished out on my behalf. I've never seen anything so hot in my life.

I run to him and he opens his arms and lifts me up, and I wrap my legs around his waist. I kiss his face all over, the smooth and the rough, and he laughs at my enthusiasm.

"Here I am, baby girl," he murmurs into my hair.

I'm so happy to finally meet the man whose voice and touch I've come to love. I don't care about the jaunty scars down his face.

"I love you," I tell him, in between planting kisses on his face.

"I love you too, baby girl." He presses his lips to mine, and in an instant I'm hot for him again, knowing what his body can make me do.

"I'm getting you away from here," he says, and I realize how the apartment block must look to him, with its crumbling brick work, peeling paint around the window frames, and scraps of litter on the shared grass areas.

"I can't leave Mom."

"She'll be taken care of. I'll send Mrs. Hughes around, and tomorrow we'll move her into a private hospital."

My eyes go wide with astonishment and he chuckles at me, a deep throaty laugh that's as strong and sexy as his voice.

"Don't worry, baby girl. I'll take care of you and your mother for the rest of your lives."

I smother him with kisses again, and he bats me off like I'm an excited puppy, but I love the smile that he gives me, lighting up his flawed but utterly perfect face.

"Get your things, quickly," he growls. "I need to make you mine properly."

11

JONATHAN

The car ride home is torture. She's still wearing her cleaning uniform, and the skirt rides up over her thighs.

I run my hand up the delicate flesh, and when I reach the hot spot it's dripping wet. I almost hit a cyclist swerving at the last moment. Chloe's so fucking distracting.

I hit the button for the gates at the bottom of the hill so I can tear right through and down the drive. I pull up in front of the house, causing stones to fly up behind the tires.

Mrs. Hughes rushes out of the front door, her arms flapping.

"I need you to go to Chloe's house and look after the woman there," I bark at her as I climb out of the car.

Mrs. Hughes doesn't bat an eyelid but goes into the house to get her things.

In two strides, I yank open the passenger door and pull Chloe out of the car. I lift her up in my arms and carry her into the house.

We pass Mrs. Hughes on the way out, and I slam the door behind me with my foot. I can smell Chloe's sweat and the sex from today, and it's making my body hot and my dick twitch, impatient to claim what's mine.

I start to carry her up the staircase, but she's wriggling against me. It's too much for me to bear.

"We're doing this now," I tell her, setting her down on the marble staircase.

Her eyes widen, and she opens her legs and leans back.

"I want you, sir."

It's like the words turn me into a wild animal. I growl as I reach between her legs and rip her panties off with one tug. I'm two steps below her, and the pink flesh of her dripping pussy makes my dick throb. I pull it out, and her eyes widen.

"I'm going in bare," I tell her. "I'm going to make you mine and plant my seed."

She nods at me, my obedient baby girl.

"You will be mine forever. Understand?"

"Yes," she says looking me straight in the eye. "I want that, too."

I reach forward and rip her blouse off, the buttons pinging down the staircase. Her breasts spill over her bra, and I pull it down so they bob free.

"Turn around for me."

She turns so she's kneeling on the stairs, her hands

pressed into the stairs a few steps above. I throw up the hem of her skirt so I can see her ass and the pink folds of her pussy. I lose my pants and straddle her, my bare thighs brushing against hers.

My hand reaches around to stroke her wet pussy. She's ready for me, and I slap my dick against her ass. I run the tip along her glistening lips, my pre-cum adding to her wetness.

I push the tip in, and she cries out.

She's so tight and hot and wet, and it feels like home.

"This is going to hurt a little," I tell her. "Just the first time, when I break your cherry. After that, it will feel good."

"It already feels good."

I ease in a little more, and *fuck*, it's so fucking tight. It's like my dick is in a hot wet vice. It feels fucking fantastic, and I can't hold back any longer. I need to be inside her.

"Brace yourself, baby girl."

I thrust hard and feel her barrier burst. The warmth gushes around me, and she cries out. I almost cum there and then. I slide back, giving her a few gentle thrusts.

This is an exercise in fucking self-control, and as soon as I hear her cries turn to moans, I let myself go.

I pump her hard, one hand squeezing her fleshy ass and pulling her to me. My dick slides in and out of her tight pussy. She lifts herself to meet me, moaning every time I push into her.

My knees are rubbing against the velvet carpet, and I pull her down a step, pushing her into its soft folds. My dick sinks in even deeper and I fuck her hard, like a man possessed. She brings a hand around to rub her clit, and I feel her pussy tighten as her climax builds.

I'm riding a wave of pure ecstasy, and one more thrust and I peak inside her, shooting hot cum into her. Claiming her, finally, as mine.

As she orgasms, her pussy clenches my dick and they pulse together. Her cries echo up and down the staircase, letting the house know she's the new mistress.

Once the throbbing subsides, I ease out of her. She turns to face me, her elbows propped up against the staircase. Sweat glistens on her body, and her eyes are glazed over. Despite the load I just shot into her, my dick starts to harden again.

"Come on." I help her up off the stairs. "Let me show you your new home."

She smiles up at me, and a wave of protectiveness runs through me. She's mine now, forever. I'll always watch over her and keep her safe.

"Can we start with the bedroom?" she asks.

"We can start with any room you like, baby girl. Because I'm going to have you in all 78 of them."

"I'd like that, sir," she says.

My dick hardens immediately, and I scoop her up into my arms.

She laughs as I carry her up the stairs and through the first door I see, into a study.

I'm going to spend the rest of my life fucking this girl in every room of this goddamn house. But very soon I'm going to take her to the chapel on the ground floor, and I'm going to confirm legally that she's mine.

I'm going to claim her as my wife, like I claimed her as my woman today.

I carry her across the threshold of the study and push the back of the door with my foot. As I sit her bare ass on the polished oak desk, the door slams shut behind us.

EPILOGUE

CHLOE

Five years later...

My feet sink into the grass as I pause in the chase. My two sons are playing hide and seek, and I'm pretending I can't see them hiding behind the bulk of their father, who's propped up on an elbow on a picnic blanket.

"Boo!" The youngest jumps out and sets off laughing on his unsteady toddler feet.

I pretend to chase him as he runs giggling in a circle and back to the presumed safety of his father. Just when he thinks he's safe, Jonathan--I finally did learn his name--shoots out an arm and swings him up into the air. My other son jumps on him, and they all three tumble together onto the lawn.

I watch them as I rub my round belly. The girl inside me kicks in protest like she can't wait to come out and join the fun.

We're picnicking in the orchard at the end of the estate. Swollen apples hang from the trees, ripe and ready to be picked. I make a mental note to tell the cook to collect them for an apple pie for supper.

Most days, this is as far as we venture out. We have everything we need in the house and on the grounds. The estate is the perfect playground for the boys.

We were married two weeks after we first met in the little stone chapel on the ground floor.

My mom was well enough to walk me down the aisle, although she had to go back to the private hospital afterwards.

She's been in remission for four years now and lives by the coast in a small mansion of her own.

My husband doesn't hide away anymore. We don't leave the estate much, but when we do, I walk proudly on his arm. He's more concerned about who's looking at me than who might be looking at him.

He takes me to the cinema in town when they're playing the old movies I love.

I put the photos upright in all the rooms. It's funny looking at him without the scar.

By conventional standards, he was a good-looking man. Strong jawline, smooth skin, offset with dark brooding eyes. But to me, he's missing something without the scars.

It's our flaws that make us truly beautiful, and my man's scarred face is beauty to me.

It represents the two different sides to him, the loving father and the beast in the bedroom.

·   ·   ·

As if reading my thoughts, he turns to me, and I know what the look in his eyes means. He's insatiable, my husband, and so am I.

I beckon to Mrs. Hughes. She helps with the children now as well as keeping the house running.

"Who wants strawberries?" she asks the children, bringing over the picnic hamper. I leave them scrambling for berries as I head back to the house. My husband will follow in a few minutes, leaving just enough time for me to slip into the maid's uniform, retrieve the duster, and choose a room. I smile to myself in anticipation.

The blouse is pulled tight over my swollen breasts, and I can't get the bottom buttons done up. The skirt rides up well above my thighs.

It's probably the last time this pregnancy I'll be able to squeeze into my old uniform. I grab the duster and head up the staircase.

At the top of the stairs, I turn left. I think I'll go to the east wing today.

I slip into the sitting room. It's the room where we had our first encounter with the plush chaise longue.

Although he kept his promise and we've tried every room in the house, I keep going back to this one. The room where I first heard his voice. The room where I first fell in love.

I swish the duster lazily over the mantelpiece until the prickles on my neck let me know he's watching. He lets me carry on for a few moments before speaking.

"Panties off. Skirt up. On your hands and knees," he barks. I comply without hesitation, a thrill running through me as my knees sink into the plush carpet.

"Close your eyes," he says.

I close my eyes, my heart racing as I wait to hear what the man of the house commands of me.

KING OF THE AIR

A curvy girl and a billionaire on a life changing train ride…

Jackson

Build an empire and retire young; that's always been the dream. But now that the time has come to hand over my business, I'm not sure I can do it. Then I see her, and I know in an instant some things are worth holding onto.

Ashleigh

When I get on the crowded train home, the last thing I expect to find is a gorgeous stranger with more than the daily commute on his mind. When he orders his private helicopter to secretly meet us at the next stop, I know he's dodging someone, and it looks like I'm along for the ride.

King of the Air is a short, steamy romance featuring an alpha male and a curvy younger woman.

GET YOUR FREE BOOK

Sign up to the Sadie King mailing list for a FREE book!

Fox in the Garden is an age gap steamy romance featuring an OTT billionaire and the younger woman he claims as his own.

It's a bonus book in the Filthy Rich Love series, exclusive to my email subscribers.

Sign up here:
authorsadieking.com/bonus-scenes

If you're already a subscriber check your latest email for the link that will take you to all the bonus content.

Wild Riders MC

This group of ex-military bikers fall hard and fall fast when they encounter the curvy women who heal their hearts.

Mountain Heroes

Steamy stories featuring the men and women from Wild Heart Mountain's Search and Rescue and Fire service.

Temptation

A damaged hero and a lost virgin in an explosive instalove retelling of the Hansel and Gretel story set in the woods of Wild Heart Mountain.

A Runaway Bride for Christmas

A snowstorm keeps this runaway bride trapped in the cabin of the mountain's biggest grump.

A Secret Baby for Christmas

Mr. Porter's Christmas takes a surprise turn when his daughter's best friend turns up with his baby.

Maple Springs

Small Town Sisters

Five curvy sister's inherit a dog hotel. But can they find love? Short and steamy instalove romance!

Candy's Café

A small-town cafe that's all heart. Meet the sister's who run it and the customer's who keep coming back.

All the Single Dads

These single dad hotties are fiercely protective and will do anything for the ones they love.

Men of Maple Mountain

These men are OTT possessive and will stop at nothing to claim the curvy innocent women they become obsessed with.

The Carter Family

Blue collar men find love with curvy girls in these quick read instalove romances.

Curvy Girls Can

Short, sweet and steamy instalove stories about sassy curvy women and the men who love them.

The Seal's Obsession

A soft stalker, secret baby, military romance. Featuring an OTT obsessed alpha male and a sassy curvy girl.

Kings County

Kings of Fire

Smoking hot tales of insta-love, featuring brave heroes and sassy heroines that will melt your heart.

King's Cops

Do you love police romance books? Then the King's Cops series is for you! Short, sweet and steamy tales of insta-love, featuring brave heroes and sassy heroines that will melt your heart.

For a full list of Sadie King's books check out her website

www.authorsadieking.com

ABOUT THE AUTHOR

Sadie King is a USA Today Best Selling Author of over 120 short and steamy contemporary romances. She loves writing about military heroes and the sassy women who heal their hearts.

Sadie lives in New Zealand with her ex-military husband and raucous young son.

When she's not writing she loves catching waves with her son, running along the beach, and drinking good wine, preferably with a book in hand.

www.authorsadieking.com

THANK YOU

Thank you for reading my story! If you enjoyed it, please consider leaving a review, they mean so much to authors and it helps other readers find books they might like.

Thank you!
Sadie xx